Charles Kerry, Thomas de Musca

The Hermitages of Depedale

Or Notes on the Chronicle of Thomas de Musca, Canon of Dale Abbey

Charles Kerry, Thomas de Musca

The Hermitages of Depedale
Or Notes on the Chronicle of Thomas de Musca, Canon of Dale Abbey

ISBN/EAN: 9783337201661

Printed in Europe, USA, Canada, Australia, Japan

Cover: Foto ©Andreas Hilbeck / pixelio.de

More available books at **www.hansebooks.com**

Depedale, and the Chronicle of Thomas de Musca, Canon of Dale Abbey

BY THE REV. CHARLES KERRY,

Curate in Charge of Stonebroom, Co. Derby.

THERE is no parish in England whose earliest recorded history dawns upon us with a greater glow of interest than the Parish of Dale Abbey. Depedale, in the county of Derby (for such was its ancient appellation) would appear to have been selected by heaven for a home of devotion, and the place, named *in vision* by the lips of the Blessed Virgin herself, has had a constraining charm for the devout as well as the curious from the time of S. Bernard until now. Seldom a day passes—and no wonder—but the quaint little village is enlivened by the feet of pilgrims, young and old, from every quarter. The place abounds with ample food for thought and profitable meditation.

Here is the veritable hermitage which has borne silent testimony for at least seven hundred years to the self-denying zeal and devotion of a poor baker of Derby ; showing how "for the sake of the hope set before him" he could leave all that was near and dear to him, and take up his cross in a lonely life of self-denial.

Here, too, is the little church founded by his friend and protectress, "The Gomme of the Dale," in which her son Richard administered the rites of the Church to his mother's little community, if not to the venerable hermit himself, before one stone of the Abbey was laid.

And here also are the scattered remains of that stately foundation which for generations was the centre of religious life in this part of the county.

The Chartulary of the Abbey, a most precious document, containing a transcript of the ancient records and title deeds of the monastery of Dale, is still preserved in the library of the British Museum (Vesp. E. xxvi. Plut. xxvi. H. (18.) The volume is a quarto of vellum, measuring 11 inches by 8, and containing 186 leaves. A page at the commencement is inscribed, "Ex dono Anchitelli Gray de Risley in Com : Derb : Armigeri." (He was living in 1701.) The first part of the MS. seems to have been written about the time of Edward I. c. 1272 ; at least as far as fol. 141, except a few lines on fol. 42b, which may have been inserted *temp.* Edward IV., forming a memorandum of certain rents received.

From fol. 141b to 167b, the MS. is in another hand, equally as early, and most beautifully written.

At fol. 168, commences the List of the Abbots of Dale.

The capitals at the commencement of each chapter are coloured red as far as fol. 104.

From fol. 178 to fol. 185 the MS. consists of fragments of a Rent Roll of the Abbey demesnes.

The Chronicle of Thomas de Musca, Canon of Dale Abbey, begins at fol. 170, and terminates abruptly with the words "et Hugo de . . . ." The hiatus, however, is supplied by Peck in his "Desiderata Curiosa," and the chronicle will be found complete in the following translation from Glover's "History of Derbyshire." The Latin version has been carefully printed from the original MS. in Caley and Ellis's edition of "Dugdale's Monasticon," Vol. vi. Pt. 2. p. 892, and is thus headed, "Ex vetusto exemplari penes Joh : Vincent, generos :" It has also been printed in full in the fifth volume of the "Journal of the Derbyshire Archæological and Natural History Society," where it is accompanied by a new and carefully-made translation.

It seems that this chronicle was once detached from the chartulary, and is alluded to in the Vol. Julius c. vii. fol. 265. Both of these are noticed in Tanner's " Notitia Monastica." There are 13 chapters composing this chronicle. The *initial* letters of all the chapters being placed together form the writer's name.

In the present paper I print the translation as given by Glover, in small type, and intersperse, where needful, descriptive, explanatory, and topographical notes in a larger type.

THE CHRONICLE OF THOMAS DE MUSCA.

CHAPTER I.

"*Assit principio Sancta Maria meo.*"

1. To thy petition my very dear brother (since it is truly virtuous and useful), being willing to accede (in order that my mind busied in the pious avocations of the sorrow lately fallen upon me may bear more lightly its burden), I will endeavour to set forth, briefly and with fidelity, in what manner Divine Piety (who selected not a people on account of a location, but a location on account of a people) looked down with mercy upon this place, and appointed it for her own indwellers,—by whom it was inhabited before the coming of our Præmonstratentians, and through whom, and in what manner our Order was, by the right hand of God planted here ; as from our predecessors, and from others who were well acquainted with what I am about to relate, I have known by veracious narrative, so that those who come after us may speak the praises of the Lord and of His power, and the wonderful things which He hath done in this place.

2. But I beseech thee, whosoever thou mayest be who shalt rend this, that thou say not of me *I presume* in attempting this little work unattempted by the illustrious men who have preceded us in our path of life ; but that thou accept it in the disposition in which I compose it. For with no impulse of any levity or temerity do I commence it, but with true humility and benevolence, that our juniors and others so inclined may have knowledge of past events done in this place in the days of our forefathers ; which, if through neglect they should not be committed to writing, might be unknown to posterity. Read therefore patiently ; and when thou shalt have perused it throughout, shouldest thou in this little work perceive certain things worthy of emendation, be, I implore you, a charitable *corrector* and not a presumptuous detector ; for never ·can he be a judicious emendator, who is at any time a sinister interpretator. Yet as there are many who delight without cause, to speak ill of the writings of the pious, I, with the invocated grace of the Holy Spirit, unterrified by such "barkings" against me, after the example of Ulysses towards the voices of the Syrens, will, with a deafened ear, go on persevering to the end.

3. May the Most High cause my name, through the merits of my readers, to be inscribed in the book of the living. To anyone desirous of knowing that name, the attainment will be easy by means of the chapter letters, the third distinction of the work being passed over.

CHAPTER II.

Concerning the friar Thomas, the abbot Iohn, and his fraternity.

1. Honourable do I esteem it in the opening of my second chapter, briefly to compose something in praise of those illustrious men who received me among them, when on the call of God I put on the Regular habit.

2. What man upon earth ought this work not to praise, whom a life of holiness has conducted to the grave, and whom Christ hath already happily crowned in the heavens?

3. Being in the middle of the flowery period of boyhood and youth given by my father to the service of God, and of His pious Virgin Mother, I took upon myself the sacred habit in this place, from the Abbot John Gauncorth, a venerable father, lovely in the eyes of God and men, who had been the especial associate of the blessed Augustine of Lavendon. [near Olney, Bucks.]

4. These two shone forth in their days and in their order like the morning and evening stars in the firmament of heaven.

5. There were at that time, men belonging to this monastery who lived before the Lord without enmity who wore vestments of virtues, who had the countenances of angels, who glowed with mutual affection, and served the Lord Jesus Christ devoutly.

6. Who is there capable of enumerating the virtues of the friar Galfrid of Sawell, of the friar Roger of Derby, or of the rest? It became such a father to have such sons.

7. Had I the abundant utterance of a Homer or a Maro, language would, I think, be inadequate to declare the magnitude of their virtues.

8. I had been four years and more a member of their congregation, when a noble matron, the Lady Matilda de Salicosa-Mara,* the foundress of our church (whose memory is constantly in our benedictions), came to us from the district of Lindsay, then aged and full of days; who, knowing that the time of her vocation from this world was approaching, had disposed herself to commend her end to God through the prayers of such holy men. Having called them together in her presence on a certain holiday for the sake of discoursing with them, and mention having been made relative to the earliest inhabitants of this place, she introduced the following narrative into her conversation with us.

CHAPTER III.

Concerning the Baker who became a Hermit: the first inhabitant of Depedale.

1. Open your ears to my words, my dearly beloved children, said she, and I will narrate unto you a fable :—no, not a fable; an event which most certainly came to pass.

2. There was a baker in Derby, in the street which is called after the name of St. Mary. At that period the church of the Blessed Virgin at Derby was the head of a large parish ; and had under its authority a church *de onere* and a chapel. And this baker, otherwise called Cornelius, was a religious man, fearing God, and moreover so wholly occupied in good works and the bestowing of alms, that whatsoever remained to him on every seventh day beyond what had been required for the food and clothing of himself and his, and the needful things of his house, he would on the Sabbath-day, take to the church of St. Mary, and give to the poor for the love of God and of the Holy Virgin.

3. And when that he had during many years led a life of such pious exercises as these, and was dear to God and accepted by him, it would please God to try him more perfectly, and having tried him to crown him with glory.

4. And therefore it happened, that on a certain day in autumn, when he had resigned himself to repose at the hour at noon, the Blessed Virgin Mary appeared to him in his sleep, saying—

5. "Acceptable in the eyes of my Son and of me, are the alms thou hast bestowed. But now, if thou art willing to be made perfect, leave all thou hast, and go to Depedale, where thou shalt serve my Son and me, in solitude ; and when thou shalt happily have terminated thy course, thou shalt inherit the

---

* See chap. xii. 8.

kimgdom of love, joy, and eternal bliss which God has prepared for those who love him."

6. The man awakening, perceived the divine goodness which had been done for his sake, and giving thanks to God and the Blessed Virgin, his encourager, he straightway went forth without speaking a word to anyone ; *with knowledge ignorant*, to use the expression of St. Benedict : *with knowledge*, because he had been taught the name of the place ; *ignorant*, because he knew not where any name of that place might be.

7. Having turned his steps towards the east, it befel him as he was passing through the middle of the village of Stanley, he heard a woman saying to a girl : "Take our calves with you : drive them as far as Depedale, and make haste back."

8. Having heard this, this man, admiring the favour of God, and believing that this word had been spoken in grace, as it were, to him, was astonished, and approached nearer and said, "Good woman, tell me, where is Depedale ?" She replied, "Go with this maiden, and she, if you desire it, will show you the place."

9. When he had arrived there, he found that the place was marshy and of fearful aspect, far distant from any habitation of man. Then directing his steps to the south-east of the place, he cut for himself in the side of the mountain, in the rock, a very small dwelling, and an altar towards the south, which hath been preserved unto this day ; and there he served God, day and night, in hunger and thirst, in cold and in meditation.

CHAPTER IV.

Concerning the tithe of the mill of Burgum [Borrowash] granted to the hermit.

1. Mighty in power of that time was a certain man, named Radulph, the son of Geremund, the lord of half the manor of Okebrook, and of Alvaston cum Soka.

2. This lord, having upon some account, returned from Normandy to England, it pleased him to visit his lands and his woods. And it came to pass, on a certain day, seeking amusement, he came with his dogs in order to hunt in his woods at Okebrook, accompanied by numerous attendants, and drew near the spot where lived the man of God ; and, observing the wretchedness of the man, he granted to him the place ; and, beholding the smoke of fire going up from the cavern of the man of God, he was greatly astonished that anyone should have the audacity to make for himself a residence in that wood without his permission.

3. Coming up to the spot, he found the man clothed in old rags and skins. And when he had enquired of him, how and whence, and for what purpose he had come there ; and when the other had explicitly shown the cause, this same Radulph, the son of Geremund, was smitten at the heart, and bestowed upon him the tithe of his mill at Burgum, for his support. And from that time even unto this day hath that tithe remained to the friars who serve God at Depedale.

4. Thus far, the Lady Matilda, aforementioned, continued her narrative. She told us also many other circumstances, which shall be detailed in their proper place.

The Radulph (de Hanseliu), the son of Geremund, here alluded to, was Seneschal of Normandy. By the marriage of his daughter Margery with Serlo de Grendon, this "Half the manor of Ockbrook" passed in dowry to the Grendons.

In chap. x. 4 of the Chronicle, we read that William, son of Serlo de Grendon, retained for himself in his lordship the serfs and the mansion of Boyhawe, which was situate in a field called "Boyhawe Meadow." "Boyhawe Grange" (now called "Boya") lies to the S.E. of the Hermitage, and about one mile from the church. It consists of a brick house of the last century, with modern farm buildings close by. The house is surrounded by a well defined quadrangular depression, indicative of an ancient moat, part of which still serves for a pond, and part for an osier bed. Within this moat was the house of "Radulph;" and from this place he set forth with his attendants on the day he found the hermit. A spot so historical must be worth a visit from every lover of Depedale. Many of the stones in the walls about the homestead exhibit the diagonal chiselling of olden times, which, if not the relics of the old "mansion of Boy-hawe," must have been brought from the Abbey.

CHAPTER V.

How it happened that he changed his place and built the chapel of the Blessed Virgin Mary.

1. And it came to pass that the old designing enemy of mankind, beholding this disciple of God flourishing with the different flowers of the virtues, began to envy him, as he envies other holy men ; sending frequently amidst his cogitations the vanities of the world, the bitterness of his existence, the solitariness of his situation, and the various troubles of the desert ; as Humfrid, and many persons now living, understood, and were accustomed to relate to me and to others.

2. This Humfrid, as he often asserted had been a tenant of the *Gomme de la Dale,* of whom mention will be made hereafter.

3. But the aforesaid man of God, conscious of the venom of the crooked serpent, did by continual prayer, repeated fastings and holy meditations, cast forth, through the grace of God, all his temptations. Whereupon the enemy rose upon him in all his might both secretly and openly, waging with him a visible conflict. And while the assaults of his foe became day by day more grievous, he had to sustain a very great want of water. Wandering about the neighbouring places, he discovered a spring, in a valley, not far from his dwelling, towards the west, and near unto it he made for himself a cottage, and built an oratory in honour of God and the Blessed Virgin. There wearing away the sufferings of his life, laudably, in the service of God, he departed happily to God, from out of the prison-house of the body.

CHAPTER VI.

Concerning the vision of the Cross that appeared to Uthlagus when he was sleeping upon Lynderyke.

1. Suffer me now to narrate that memorable event, so well known by our forefathers, which, about the same period, God deigned to manifest in this place by his immediate ministry.

2. There was one Uthlagus, a very famous man, who frequented these parts, on account of the passage of wayfarers through the forest between Nottingham and Derby ; for the whole country between the bridge of Derby and the water of....... was at that time covered with wood.

3. And it came to pass, on one of the days of the summer season, this Uthlagus was sitting upon Lynderyke, which is a hill, westward of the gate of our monastery, with his companions amusing themselves around him, when a deep sleep fell upon him. And, while he slept, he saw in his dream, a golden cross, standing in that spot where the foundation of our church is laid, the top of which touched the heavens ; while the extremities of the arms stretched themselves on each side, even unto the ends of the world. And, moreover, he beheld men coming from the various nations of the earth, and most devoutly adoring the cross.

4. The man being aroused and awakened from his sleep, called together his companions and related to them the vision that had been revealed to him from the Lord : and he added and said, "Truly, my dearly beloved companions, the valley which ye behold below, and which is contiguous to this eminence, is a holy place." "Of a truth," he said again, "the Lord is in this place, and I knew him not. Children shall be born and shall grow up, and shall declare to their children the wonderful works that the Lord will perform in this valley. This valley I say unto you, shall be white with the flowers of the virtues, and shall be filled with delights and with plenteousness. For there shall come as it has been revealed to me, from various nations, to worship the Lord, in this valley, and to serve him, until the end

of time through the succession of ages.   And because our Lord Jesus Christ hath
deigned to show to me, a sinner, his secret intentions, so shall ye understand that
ye can no longer have in me either a companion or a leader ; but, aided by his
grace, I will amend my life according to his will."

5. Then embracing them every one, he turned himself away from them ; but
whither he went, nought was known at that time concerning him.

6. Some there were who said he went to Depedale, and there in secret
intercourse served the Lord, and with a peaceful end came to rest in the Lord.

THE HERMITAGE, whose formation by Cornelius, the baker-hermit,
has been detailed in the third chapter, may be considered the germ
of the subsequent glories of Dale.   The self-denying life of the
hermit soon bore fruit in the solitudes of Depedale.   By a sort of
attractive power the cell became the centre of spiritual life and devotion ; and in a little while, in the language of the prophet, " The
wilderness and the solitary place became glad for them, and the
desert rejoiced, and did blossom as the rose."

The Hermitage is excavated in an elevation of soft sandstone, which
forms the southern boundary of the Dale.   It consists at the present
time of one apartment, measuring about six yards by three, which is
entered by a doorway between two window holes.   One of these (the
western) has been formed out of a doorway ; and there can be no
doubt but that originally the cell was divided into *two* compartments,
the one towards the west forming the oratory, and the other with
the present doorway and adjacent window east of it, the ordinary abode
of the hermit.

From the description of the Hermitage in the last section of the
third chapter it seems that the hermit built his altar " *towards the
south ;* " that is, opposite the door of the oratory.

From this it must be inferred that the smaller of the two apart-
ments (the one to the west, with the half-blocked door) was the room
set apart for devotion, the *narrowness* of the place preventing the
usual eastward arrangement.   Close by, in the western wall, may still
be seen a niche, as if for a lamp or some such thing.   There is a
similar niche with a small oil dish, for a light, hewn in its stone sill, in
the narrow oratory of St. Cuthbert, beneath Hexham Abbey Church.

There are other holes here and there in the walls, which, it is to be
feared, are of no great antiquity, for the place has served other pur-
poses than those of austere seclusion and devotion.

About seventy years ago, it was actually occupied by one of the
inhabitants of the village during the rebuilding of his cottage, and
here too he erected his stocking-frame !   But this is not all ; in this
very place his wife presented her spouse with a son !

The fire-place was constructed in the N.E. corner, and the careful
observer may discover the blocked chimney-vent.   The " stopping "
has been judiciously done, and time has harmonised the work with its
surroundings.

The Hermitage has had another providential escape.   Mr. Chand-
ler, a former steward of this estate, gave permission to one. William
McConnell to furnish the Hermitage with a door and windows, so as
to enable him to extort a fee from visitors for its exhibition.   For-
tunately, the man died before he could accomplish his design.

It is much to be regretted that some visitors should think it necessary to disfigure the rocky walls of the Hermitage with their initials ;
much better to perpetuate their memories by some good or generous
action, for then their names would probably be written in a record
which time can never efface.   Who cares to see ⎾S. I.⏌, or ⎾M. P. L.⏌,
or ⎾E. T.⏌, or ⎾O. N.⏌ carved in such a place ? but it may be a useful
lesson for the cutters to learn, that many who look on these precious
memorials consider the initials to be connected in some way or other
with the old English word " *Fool*."

The view of the Abbey from the Hermitage in the days of its pros-
perity must have been very striking ; and it was, undoubtedly, a
favourite resort, not only for strangers, but also for the " Religious "
themselves.

A capacious seat, hewn in the adjoining rock to the east, is very sug-
gestive.   It requires but little effort of the imagination to picture
some aged member of the fraternity, in his white cassock and scapular,
gazing from this resting place on his conventual home—and a beautiful scene it was.   Towering above all stood the church, its chiefest
glory.   The choir, nave, and transepts formed a grand cross with a
lofty tower at the intersection.

On the south side of the choir lay an aisle with a south chapel
annexed, both terminating westward in the transept.   There was a
chapel also on the east side of the north transept, but this was not
visible from the Hermitage, being concealed by the high roof of the
choir.   Nearer still lay the group of buildings round the cloister
square.   The nave formed its northern boundary.   On the east side lay
the south transept, the sacristies, the chapter-house, and the calefac-
tory, divided from the former by a passage called the " slype."   On the
south side was the refectory, or dining-room, covered in later times
with a heavy debased roof of oak, and lighted by a series of flat-
headed windows, all richly dight with stories and legends of old*.
Next came the kitchen and other offices.   The remaining side to the
west was the hall of the conversi, or lay members of the confraternity.
Westward still lay the gateway with the slopes of " Lynderwyke "
rising beyond.

The fifth chapter of the Chronicle, here given, is most important,
and leads me to the consideration of the " SECOND HERMITAGE," or
Parish Church, of Dale Abbey.

From chapters iv. and v. of the Chronicle we learn that after Ralph
de Hanselin, the son of Germund, Lord of Ockbrook, had granted the
tithe of his mill at Borrowash to the hermit of Depedale, the recluse
left his cavern, and erected an oratory, with a dwelling for himself, near
a spring, a little to the west of his former cheerless abode.   At this
very time there is a spring a " little to the west " of the hermitage
still called " The Hermit's Well."   It is not now seen bubbling from
its original source, for that is covered by the *debris* worked down and
trodden in from the sides of the original channel by the hoofs of cattle

* The roof and windows of the refectory may be seen in the north aisle at Morley
Church.

through many long ages. The bed of the depression is now a quag-mire, producing a luxuriant crop of watercress; but in the midst of it is a shallow stone-girt well of no great antiquity, the top of which affords a firm footing to the visitor. The spring is certainly in its ancient position, for natural features are slow to change. A few yards west of this spring is the church, with a dwelling-house adjoin-ing. There is probably no other church in the kingdom so much at one with a domestic edifice, and it is this feature which leads the writer to think that both church and house relatively occupy the identical sites of the oratory and dwelling *erected* by the hermit.

The Chronicle further informs us that Serlo de Grendon, who married the daughter of the above-mentioned Ralph, gave Depedale to his godmother; thus placing the hermit and his *buildings* under the patronage of this devout woman, who was known from henceforth as the Gomme (or "Godmother") of the Dale. "And, moreover, the mansion of this same matron was on the *higher land eastward of us, inclining to the south,* where there is now a pond which is called the pond of Roger de Alesby. When our fathers dug out that pond they found at the bottom many wrought stones which had formerly belonged to the above-mentioned mansion." It would perhaps be difficult now to decide which was the pond of Roger de Alesby, but if the moat or pond at Boyhaw Grange be not the water referred to, which I certainly think most probable, then there are two which come within the bearings indicated; one lying at the bottom of the small field adjoining the churchyard on the west, and the other near the south-east corner of the Abbey-field; this was associated in more recent times with a tanyard. The former, being nearer the church, has, I think, prior claims, although the latter seems more in the right direction.

Let us now see whether we can find any evidence in the present buildings of the truth of these statements of Thomas de Musca with regard to their origin.

In the 3rd section of the fifth chapter we have mention of an "oratory" with a "cottage;" that is, an oratory *built by* a man who was originally *a baker* in S. Mary's Street, in Derby. He was not a *mason,* but a *baker.* His oratory would naturally be of a simple and unarchitectural character as such an unskilful workman would build—probably of unhewn stones, with a preponderance of timber—in fact, no very durable structure but such a building as might perhaps last a hundred years or more.

The oratory would now undoubtedly be placed to the *east* of his dwelling, with the door at its western end, if both struc-tures were under one continuous roof. It is my firm belief that the *south aisle* of the church occupies the *very site* of the original oratory built by the hermit, though its *present* walls were not constructed until at least 150 years after his death. But I am forestalling my subject. I must refer to the period at which the grant of Depedale was made to the Godmother of Serlo de Grendon. At that time there were standing the oratory and the cottage of Cornelius. "Now" (in the words of the Chronicle), "she had a son named Richard, a youth of good disposition; whom, when he had studied the sacred writings, and after that he had duly taken Holy Orders, she caused to be ordained a priest, with the purpose that he should assist in divine service in *her* chapel of Depedale; and such ministry he performed." "*Her* chapel;" what does this mean? Does she call the hermit's oratory "*her* chapel?" or, has she erected a new building for herself and hers which might be more correctly termed "her chapel?" I think so, for if the hermit was living she would not wish to thrust the devotee out of his retreat, nor would his ministrations, being a *layman*, in any degree fulfil her ecclesiastical requirements. It may be concluded, therefore, that, with the view of her son Richard's ordination, she erected a chapel for herself and her people, independent of the original oratory.

It is not likely, even were the hermit dead, that she would ruthlessly lay violent hands on the sacred but humble retreat of the recluse consecrated by so much devotion, but rather would seek *to attach her new chapel to his oratory*, so as to place her sanctuary under the shadow of a building consecrated by so much devotion. This course would be in accordance with the religious spirit of those times.

Hence, it may be inferred that the oratory of the hermit and the new chapel of the Gomme stood *side by side*—the chapel of the Gomme, a Norman structure; the oratory of the hermit, a rude building, with no particular architectural features, having his residence at its western end. There could be no reason why the two buildings should not be thrown into one; every reason to the contrary. A hermit surely (if living) would not object to a canonical service; and, if dead, it would be the more desirable to unite such a shrine to the House of God.

Now observe. There are *indications of a Norman arcade* between the nave and south aisle (built c. 1150), of which a fragment of an abacus of that date may be seen on the impost between the chancel and the south aisle. Added to this, there is a corresponding abutment erected to resist the lateral thrust of this arcade on the outer face of the western wall, but now concealed by the dwelling house. The doorway of the nave is of the same early character, and these features indicate the erection of the nave and chancel at that period.

Again. *This portion* of the church was clearly the work of the "Gomme of the Dale," because her chapel, *designed* for *Sacramental* rites, would require accommodation for their due performance, and so *the Chancel must have been provided at that time.*

There are no traces of Norman work in the south aisle; it seems to have been entirely reconstructed about 1250. The western doorway of this aisle (now blocked) is of the same period too. It has a plain chamfer round its western margin. If this portion was originally built at the same time as the arcade (1150), why should it require *reconstruction* so soon? The arcade *alone* proves a building to have stood on the south side the nave in 1150, and in 1250 that building (if erected in 1150) would be only 100 years old. How can we account for its speedy demolition, unless we suppose it to have been the simple oratory erected by the hermit, which by that time would undoubtedly require reconstruction.   As a confirmation of this theory, it may be observed that *the floor of the south aisle is much higher* than that of the nave, indicating its former detached condition.

It is quite certain that the south aisle was separated from the nave about 1480, for the framework or screen of that period *now existing* exhibits the grooves of the original panelling.   There was a small doorway at its western end.

To resume.   In or about 1150, the present nave and chancel of the church were added to the original oratory, which was erected by the hermit Cornelius a few years before.

The oratory, or south aisle, falling into decay, was entirely rebuilt about the year 1250.   At the same time two larger windows were inserted in the chancel—of these the characteristic splays are now the only indications.   An engaged shaft or column ran up the outer angle of each splay of the east window—these would probably support an inner drop arch beneath the window head.   Thus the church remained until about 1480, when it underwent a transformation.

The reader must imagine the church up to this date to have had two parallel roofs, and consequently, two gables towards the east and two towards the west.   The date of the roodscreen gives the clue to the time of these alterations.   When that was formed, the Norman arcade between the nave and south aisle was removed ; for *the screne terminates in the centre line* of the old arcade.   The destruction of this middle masonry naturally necessitated a change in the roof-plan.   The two western gables near the house were taken down to some distance below the eaves, and the whole of the church walls were reduced to the same level !   The line of decapitation cut off the heads of the lancets in the south aisle, as well as swept away the tracery of the windows of the chancel ; the two last were then filled with windows of late Perpendicular character.   The debased head of the east window shows the former *vertical* angle-shafts carried over the arch.

The united width of nave and aisle being now greater than the length, a sort of upper storey was constructed above them, with the roof line stretching *from north to south*.   In this roof, that of the chancel as well as the house on the opposite side, was made to terminate,

The gallery over the *nave* is clearly co-eval with the roodscreen, and partly rests upon it.   It has always been approached from the south aisle.   It has a level plaister floor beneath the boarding.   The continuation of this gallery southwards over the south aisle must have been a later work, and may have been done as early as 1651.

Monuments.—At the west end of the aisle stands a large incised slab of alabaster, removed some years ago from beneath a pew on the north side of the chancel.   It bears indications of four male figures of civilians beneath a continuous canopy.   All that can now be deciphered of the marginal inscription is—

✠ 𝔒rate pro aiabus 𝔓etri 𝔑esse, 𝔠home 𝔕ogers,
𝔍ohis ✠ 𝔐id......✠......𝔐. 𝔇. xxx. ii. ✠

The crosses occur at the angles of the stone.

A marble tablet on the south side of the chancel is inscribed—

IN MEMORY OF
JOHN STEVENS
LATE OF BOYA GRANGE IN THIS PARISH
WHO DIED APRIL 1. 1838,
AGED 61 YEARS.

A tablet on the north wall has—

"Sacred
to the memory of the
Right Hon. Philip Henry,
Earl Stanhope,
of Chevening in Kent,
Lord of this manor,
and
Lay Bishop of this church,
who died March 2, 1855,
aged 78 years.
This tablet is erected by the
Parishioners of Dale Abbey."

The altar has been converted into a cupboard, which is still a useful repository. About thirty years ago, it contained the parish registers. The following account of them was written at that time :—" The oldest register is in a deplorable condition. Being of paper, the mice have eaten a hole in the centre of the first few leaves. The margins are much frayed, and several entries have been abstracted. The oldest register extends from 1670 to 1729. The second book is of parchment, and is in good preservation. The third is of paper, with a parchment cover." It is only just to add that these valuable documents are now carefully preserved, in a "safe," by the present rector.

The *Chalice* is probably one of the largest in England. Its dimensions are :—Height, 9 inches ; depth of bowl, 6 in. ; circumference at rim, 14 in. ; do. at base, 10½ in.; circumference of stem, 5in. Round the bowl is inscribed—" *Dale Abby Communion Bowle.*" In the hollow of the base—" *Given by ye Honorable Anchitell Gray, 1701.*"

The *Font* is one of the most interesting relics the church contains. It undoubtedly adorned the Abbey Church before the Dissolution, and was allowed to remain in the sacred precincts whilst its surroundings were gradually swept away. It is more than probable that the beautiful carvings of the Crucifix, and of the Virgin and Child, which adorn two of its sides, have contributed in no small degree to its preservation. The font was removed from the village many years ago to Stanton Hall by Mr. Woodward, a former steward, where it served for a flower vase on the lawn. About twelve years ago it was brought back to its ancient home by Mr. John Hancock, and placed in the churchyard. The growing reverence for holy things has conveyed it within the sanctuary, and it is used once more for the hallowed purpose for which it was designed of old. It consists of a large octagonal bowl, supported by a square pedestal, which has a shallow engaged column at each angle. Five of the sides (and perhaps six, for one is concealed by a pew), are adorned with shields defined only by a cavetto. One of these has a cross saltire; the others are plain. At the bottom of each side is a rose. This rose, so like the " Tudor Rose," would almost determine the font to be of the time of Hen. VII. at the earliest; but the acutely pointed shields, as well as the "solleret " form of the feet of the Blessed Virgin, to say nothing of the high art, and the exquisite feeling in the treatment of the figures, compel me to assign this beautiful font to the time of Hen. VI.—say, 1440—1460. The head of our Lord on the cross, as well as the head of the B.V.M. and the Divine Child, have been mutilated ; indeed, the Infant has all but disappeared.

THE CHURCH HOUSE.—It is probable that *before* the year 1480 (an approximate date) the house was altogether detached from the church, as the old buttress at the west end would seem to indicate. It is also probable that it terminated in a line with the present centre chimney block, and that the stone foundation, with its chamfer at the western or parlour end, denotes the extent of the original house of Richard, the chaplain.

In 1480, the old house was *entirely* rebuilt of half-timbered work, and joined on to the church by a new wing, this new extension, forming the present kitchen, but then limited to the width of the south aisle, the old buttress not being inclosed. The union of the house with the church at this time is proved by a window hole of this date between the bedroom and the upper storey of the south aisle. The position of this opening seems to indicate that the daily mass instituted by Serlo de Grendon was said in the south aisle ; that is, in the hermitage chapel proper, and not in the chancel. This communication between the house and the church would indicate a desire on the part of the occupants of the bed-chamber to hear Divine service. It is, therefore, not unlikely that the house of 1480 may have been used for an infirmary by the monastics. Only two walls remain of the house of 1480—viz., the west end and the western half of the north front. All the rest is the work of 1651. This includes—

1. The whole of the south side of panel framing.

2. The north wall of the kitchen now set out in a line with the old parlour front, and enclosing the buttress. (The old *return* of the parlour angle at the north doorway may be seen from the mortises on the *underside* of the beam above the foot of the stairs.)

8. The double chimney stack, as appears from the date on the mantel beam within the parlour.

4. The bedroom floors. (Notice the bracket supports within the parlour, showing that the floor and joists are not co-eval with the walls.)

5. The whole of the roof, and a mud wall ("wattle and daub") between the bedroom and the church wall.

In other words, in 1651, the house was brought exactly into its present form.

CHAPTER VII.

Concerning the noble Matron who was called " The Gomme of the Dale," and of Richard, her son.

1. **D**ominus de Bradleye, the lord of Bradleye, by name Serlo de Grendon, a soldier intrepid in arms, illustrious by the eminence of his race, received Margery, the daughter of the aforesaid Radulph, the son of Geremund, as his wife, and with her the half of the Manor of Okebroke in free dowry.

2. By her he had three daughters ; viz.: Johanna, Isolda, and Agatha, to whom (with grief be it spoken), the inheritance ultimately descended.

3. He also begat five sons ; Bartholomew, who was afterwards canon with us, William, of cherished memory, our advocate ; Fulcher, Jordan, and Serlo.

4. Afterwards he married Matilda, noble by family, but still more noble by conduct, the lady of the manor of Celston.

5. By her he had Andrew of Grendon, and Ranulph, the lord of Boleston, with their brothers, who were soldiers.

6. He also had Robert, by a concubine, who was more powerful in arms than the others.

7. In that time the Grendons of that generation were men of power, the most famous of the earth.

8. Now, the Serlo already named, had a friend, who was also his spiritual mother, inasmuch as she had vowed for him in his name at the holy font.

9. To her the lord Serlo assigned the place of Depedale, with all that appertained thereunto, that she might dwell there with the whole of the land, cultivated and waste, which is between the pathway, which extends from the northern part of Boyhawe towards the west, even unto Le Colkey Sicke and Brunesbroc.

10. And because such spiritual mothers are in English called Gommes (or Godmothers), this lady herself was known by the vulgar denomination of *" Gomme of the Dale."*

11. She had a son named Richard, a youth of good disposition, whom, when he had studied the sacred writings, and after that he had duly taken holy orders, she caused to be ordained a priest, with the purpose that he should assist in Divine Service in her chapel of Depedale, and such ministry he performed.

12. And moreover, the mansion of this same matron was on the higher land eastwood of us, inclining to the south, where there is now a pond which is called the pond of Roger de Alesby. (vid. chap xiii. 5.)

13. When our fathers dug out that pond they found at the bottom many wrought stones which had formerly belonged to the above-mentioned mansion.

CHAPTER VIII.

Concerning the arrival of the Black Canons de la Kalc [Calke.]

1. **E**ven at that time when the house of Kalc had been the mother of the church at Repyndon, God, who disposes all things, being willing more gloriously to exalt the place of Depedale, the aforesaid Serlo de Grendon called together the canons of Kalc, and gave them the place of Depedale, the venerable matron having consented thereto, or rather having solicited for their coming.

2. And the chaplain, Richard, took the habit of Regulars among them. Moreover (as Humfrid, of whom I have made previous mention, hath told me), the Prior of these very canons was called Humfrid. He had two associates, Nicholas and Simon, who had been a short time before schoolfellows and companions of William de Grendon, besides the chaplain, Richard, just named, and two others, whose names have escaped my memory. This same Humfrid, with his canons, continued through days and years in this condition.

3. These aforesaid canons, having taken root in this soil, and being comforted by God, they built for themselves a church—a costly labour, and other offices.*

4. Humfrid, also their prior, visited the Roman See, and obtained a most valuable privilege, which we still hold in our possession, relative to a confirmation

---

* Perhaps the only remaining fragment of this " costly labour " is a stone, with the double chevron and beak mouldings, in the south foundation of Mr. Wright's barn, near the windmill ; it seems to have formed part of the *side* of a doorway (a. 1160).

of the right of sepulture, a chantry, the laying of interdiction upon land, and many other liberties.

5. About the same time flourished Albinus, abbot of Derley, brightly manifesting so many of the requisites of a holy and virtuous life, that the interior of the cloisters and of the church, and the most inward sanctuary of religion may be perceived to this day to be redolent with the fragrance of such a father.

6. Then began, not those only of the race of the Grendons, but many others, noble and simple, to frequent the place of Depedale, to endow it largely with their goods, and at their decease, to leave their bodies to be buried there. I have heard it said by a man of veracity, worthy of belief, that more than four hundred warriors lie buried in that place, setting aside others of the nobility and gentry, and a prodigious number of common people.

7. In the same spot reposes Peter Cook, of Batheley, a hermit of that place, a man of sanctified memory, of whose holy conversation, with which in part I was myself acquainted, and of whose actions, revealed in full confidence, by himself and by others, mention shall be made, by the aid of God, in my future works. And thus devout honour and reverence are due to the place itself, on account of its own sanctity, and on account of the bodies of Christ's faithful people who repose there.

CHAPTER IX.

Concerning the departure of the Black Canons.

1. Many were the circles of the years during which the aforesaid canons remained together in this appointed place, in distant congregation from the social intercourse of mankind; and to them, thus secluded, the pleasant aspect of the spot was delightful, and they began to hold themselves more remissly to the service of God, and to the observance of order. For they frequented the forest more than the church; were more intent upon the amusement, than the improvement of their minds; and to hunting, than to prayer or holy meditation. And, the whole of the neighbouring country being then a royal forest, as has already been stated, the king, hearing of the trespass they committed, ordered them to be removed from the place for the preservation of his deer.

2. Then they, resigning everything they possessed into the hands of their patron (William de Grendon), returned to the place from whence they came: and which they were by necessity compelled to do: but their Prior, Humfrid, betook himself to Le Magdalen, and there for many years he lived the life of a hermit.

3. Truly, for my own part, I cannot believe that all this came to pass accidentally, but that it proceeded by the will of Him, without Whom not the leaf of a tree, nor a sparrow falleth to the ground. Oh, the height of the wisdom and knowledge of God! How incomprehensible are His judgments, and how unsearchable are His ways! For who hath known the design of the Lord, or who hath been His counsellor.

4. But the place which he had chosen (see chap. vi.) the Lord would not leave thus desolate: for

" The Divine power displayeth itself in things adverse."

Little by little, His clemency began to stretch forth the hand of compassion, to greater and more wonderful things, so as that having plucked up the sycamores, he might plant cedars; instead of the Black Præmonstratensians who had quitted the place, leading hither, and establishing the White Præmonstratensians, as will be presently declared after the next chapter.

CHAPTER X.

Of the coming of the Canons of Tupholme, and of their departure.

1. Verily, there came from Tupholme, which monastery is of our order, six Canons to tarry at Depedale, being invited by the Advocate of the place (Will. de Grendon).

2. And there was given unto them the park of Stanleye, in addition to their possessions; but by whom, and in what manner, I know only in part, and altogether with uncertainty; and to write uncertain things for certain, in matters where the truth of any affair is to be treated, I hold to be absurd.

3. This indeed I know most certainly, that a convert Friar, who came with

those of Tupholme, was the first who constructed the watermill* in the park, and completed the pool with great labour and trouble.

4. Their Prior was named Henry. It was necessary for them to be, as indeed they were, extremely laborious, for they were much incommoded by the frequent visits of the keepers of the forests, and of others; nor did they possess any cultivated land, which had previously belonged to the Gomme of the Dale, already mentioned, nor Makkemore, which contained one small hide of land. The lord of Okebroke retained for himself in his lordship the serfs and the mansion of Boyhawe, which was situate in a field, now called "Boyhawe Meadow."

5. When they had sojourned here for the space of seven years, in great poverty, they sold the upper timber of the oaks in the park, which they felled at the middle of the trunks, and having received the money, they returned to Tupholme; their Abbot having recalled them.

6. As for the aforesaid Henry, their Prior, he was very cunning in the fabrication of false money, having exercised himself in that unhappy trade: he went from them to Toftweyth, and there cohabited with a certain young woman of Morley, whom he had previously known with the insane affection of filthy lust.

7. His Abbot having heard of this, and being displeased that he had neglected to return home with the brethren at his command, sent persons of the monastery and others with them, to bring him to Tupholme by force, that his disobedience and incontinence, as well as his other crimes, might be punished as they deserved, according to the ordinances of the monastery. He being seized with great affliction of the heart, was so instigated by diabolical resolution, that in a hot bath, he bled himself in both arms, and thus by a voluntary, or rather, an insane death he terminated his life.†

CHAPER XI.

Concerning the arrival of the Canons of Wellebeck, and of their departure.

1. Solitary, stained, and sallow, sat that daughter of Sion, the church of Depedale, bereft for a period of inhabitants; but the Father of mercies, and the God of all consolation, who had in His pity selected that place, again looked down upon it with an eye of clemency, and consoled it.

2. Therefore, lest that place, beloved by God, and venerable to man (the name of which through the prerogatives of its merits, is, as it were, honey melting in the mouth), should any longer be defrauded of its religious observances, He sent and caused five canons of Wellebeck, of the Præmonstratensian Order, to be brought hither.

3. The prior was named (*Boniface?*) under the abbot Richard de Sewelle; he was a man esteemed, expert in civil and religious affairs, and was afterward appointed prior to their establishment at Wellebeck; and there was also the friar William, of Hogneby, then a canon of their church, but afterwards a prior of this holy congregation, who, when I took the habit of the order, was accustomed to relate to us many circumstances respecting himself for our edification.

4. These five persons remained here, in all the severe discipline of their order, for five years in the greatest poverty, having endured in that space of time, many and varied calamities.

---

* The mill stands immediately below the railway station at West Hallam. It is termed "Bordock Mill," and undoubtedly derives its name from a "Broad Oak" which in early times grew near it. The water is gathered for some distance up the valley near Stanley Grange, and the mill is snugly esconced under the large embankment. A few of the old stones remain incorporated with brickwork of the last century. The doorway looks older, and may have been erected c. 1600.

† One of the windows of Morley Church which once adorned the Refectory of Dale Abbey has the representation of a monk manacled, and standing before his superior, who is reading some homily to him from a book. The legend beneath interprets the scene:—"*Take heed to thy ways, brother.*" There can be no doubt that this picture represents Prior Henry before his superior at Tupholme. It is probable, too, that so disgraceful an incident in the history of the convent was pourtrayed in the windows of the Refectory that it might afford a wholesome warning to the brotherhood of the grievous end of one who presumed to violate his sacred vows of poverty, obedience, and chastity.

5. And it came to pass, that on a certain day, one of them being desirous to draw up the lamps which were suspended before the altar, they all, falling to the ground, in a wonderful manner were broken into fragments.   The prior being called into the auditory, and having received permission to speak, said, amongst other matters, "Let us depart hence, since nothing happens prosperous to us, but all things go contrary to our hopes ; and truly I declare that the Lord hath judged us unworthy of this place, or perhaps hath reserved us for other and better things."   And that his words became the true prophecies of what was to happen, the following chapter will set forth, as the conclusion of this affair will show.

6. A short time afterwards, the abbot already mentioned (Richard de Sewell) came to Depedale, as he had done before, for the purpose of visiting his friars, being desirous that all things should be right with them.   And he found them enduring a life of severe poverty, possessing very little corn or meal, and still less, fresh meat.

7. The man of God, commiserating their distress, declared that he felt himself to have been unkind, and unjust, insomuch that his brethren were perishing with hunger and wretchedness in the desert, while he might have provided them sufficiently with necessary food and clothing at home, as was required by their regulation and order.

8. And when he had returned to his monastery, he discussed the matter seriously with the brethren, and, taking the advice of the most prudent, he called home the aforesaid brethren, who were residing at Depedale.

CHAPTER XII.

In what manner the manor of Stanleye, with its parish, was given to the Canons of Newhouse, by Galfrid de Salicosa-Mara, and Matilda, his wife.

1. Co-existent with these events, it came to pass that William, the son of Radulph, of whom I have already made mention (chap. iv. 1.), purchased the manor of Stanleye, from Nicholas, the son of William Chylde, of Trowell, subject to the service of the fourth part of the arming of one soldier during scutage (*i.e.*, when required.)

2. The same Nicholas held Trowell, Broculstowe, Bramcote and Staneleye, of the Lord of Kyme, by the tenure of one scutage, each of which manors were assessed to find one fourth of a scutage.*

3. And the aforesaid Nicholas held many other lands, viz., Claxton, Hewes, Leka, and Stanford, of which it is best at present to say nothing, because they have no relation to the matter of which I am treating.

4. The said William, indeed, had known that the manor of Staneley was given to Galfrid de Salicosa-Mara, who had espoused his daughter Matilda.   Then did these two, Galfrid and his spouse Matilda, having made a vow to God, present themselves before their superior lord (William de Hanselyn, their father), saying, "Thou knowest, my lord, that we have lived together in wedlock for these seven years, and more ; and that God hath deprived us of the fruit of our marriage-bed, and that we are without the comfort of children.   And, therefore, we earnestly beseech you, that with respect to the manor of Staneleye, which you have proposed to bestow on us, that you consent that we offer it to God, and confer it upon the abbot of the religious order of Præmonstratensians, who are founding a monastic house in your park, and may God, the Most High, the retributer of good deeds, looking down upon the pious devotion of your humility, grant to us the blessing

---

* Scutage, or Escuage.   Lat., *Scutagium*; Fr., *Escu* ; a shield—a kind of knight's service, called " service of the shield," whereby the tenant was bound to follow his lord into the wars at his own charge.   Also that duty or payment which they who held lands under this tenure were bound to make to the lord, when they neither went to the wars, nor provided any other in their place; being in lieu of all services. Sometimes Escuage signified a reasonable aid, demanded and levied by the lord of his tenants who held in knight-service.   Scutage was a tax on those who held land by knight-service towards furnishing the king's army.   A scutage was granted to Henry III. for his voyage to the Holy Land, of three marks on every knight's fee. It was frequently levied by the Norman and early Plantagenet Kings of England.— Vide Jacob's " Law Dictionary."

of wished-for progeny, and, on account of this benefaction, grant to us and to you the bliss of eternal life.

5. Then this nobleman understood that their hearts and counsels were inspired by God, and accordingly, beneficently yielding to their just and virtuous petitions, he caused William de Grendon, a priest, the son of his sister, and Lord of Oke-broke, to be called to him, and said to him—

6. " I propose to build a certain Monastery of the order of the Præmonstraten-sians, by the advice of my friends, in my park, at Stanleye, a place contiguous to that of Depedale, of which you are the patron, and where three congregations of different men have successively flourished, all of whom, being attacked and driven away by intolerable poverty, have left the spot desolate. And I most truly am persuaded that you will bestow that place upon my new establishment, so that between me and thee, we may provide out of our lands, possessions and goods, which God hath granted us (should God grant us length of life), that the religious men, who shall be called thither, may not be compelled by necessity to beg, or to change their situation.

7. To whom William de Grendon replied, "Blessed be the name of the Lord, who hath inspired you with so pious a purpose ! and blessed by God may they be who have given you this counsel ! so may you speedily take in hand, happily, in the name of the Lord, that which thou hast in thy mind, if it so pleaseth thee, particularly as men are so frail and mortal. And I will bestow the place of Depe-dale and all the appurtenances which are mine to grant : and never at any former period were the inhabitants of that place, whether black or white canons dwelling there, located there with more certain hope of fruitful grace. Yet I grant this place on one condition—that a priest of that congregation, shall, every day in per-petuity within the chapel of Depedale (which they must keep in repair) celebrate mass for my soul, and for the souls of my ancestors and successors, and for the souls of all those that are at rest in Christ ; and further, that upon the great table in the Refectory there shall be placed one loaf of conventual bread, beer, and money (companagi) to be distributed to the poor."

8. The nobleman, his uncle, answered him with thanks for his concessions, and said, " And I also will command and effect, that all these things shall be inviolably executed in perpetuity. And, since I, being occupied both beyond sea and at home in the business of the king, cannot find time to attend to the founda-tion of the monastery proposed in this matter, I have granted the superintendence to Galfrid de Salicosa-Mara,* and to Matilda, my daughter, his wife, and I appoint them my executors in this matter ; namely, the foundation of the monas-tery, and the recalling of the canons."

CHAPTER XIII.

Concerning the arrival of the Canons of Newhouse.

1. And having received charters and other instruments necessary for the foun-dation of the monastery from the aforesaid nobleman William, the said Galfrid and Matilda went at his command to Newhouse, that they might thence lead forth a convent.

2. For there were men in that monastery fragrant with the flowers of virtues, so that they had the rose of the firmest patience, the lily of chastity, and particu-larly the violet of the contemplation of celestial life, whom the sincerity of life and the virtue of manners so honoured, that from sea to sea, throughout all the districts of the English Kingdom, their sanctity sent abroad its odour.

3. Then the aforesaid Galfrid and Matilda arriving at Newhouse, found there the Abbot, Lambert by name, a man of the highest prudence, true to his word, just in his judgment, provident in counsel, faithful in his trust, determined in his discipline, conspicuous in beneficence, and illustrious for the universal virtue of his conduct, who so instructed his monks in the sweetness of celestial inter-course, that I may truly say with the Apostle, " Our conversation is in heaven."

---

* This Galfrid or Geoffry is mentioned in the "Testa de Nevil," a record of feudal tenants drawn up about 1272 :—
"The Soke of Gatton (Lincolns.) is escheated to our Lord the King, and is valued at £25 per annum : and Geoffry de Salicosa Mara held it of the gift of King John."

4. Galfrid and Matilda being honourably received by the aforesaid venerable father, and having explained their business and the cause of their coming, the Abbot having held a council with the brethren, granted to them that they should lead forth nine canons to Depedale, and establish the order in that place.

5. Amongst these were:—Walter de Totenhaye, a man of the highest piety, who, previously proceeding to two other places, viz., to S. Agatha and the convent of Newhouse, had founded there the same order; also John of Byford, the son of Baldwin of Byford, who was the associate of Peter de Gausila, who also was one of the founders of Newhouse; and Hugh of Grimmesby, and Roger of Alesby, and William le Sores, men of virtuous lives and great piety; together with other men of God.

6. These, O Dale, were thy living stones, thy chosen stones, the stones precious in the foundation of thy church; which stones are jointed with that Mighty Corner Stone, our Lord Jesus Christ.

THE ABBOTS OF DALE, FROM THE CHARTULARY.

1. Walter de Senteney (S. Entenne), ruled 31 years, 8 months.
2. William, a thoroughly prudent man. Ruled 2 years, 6 months, and was afterwards made Abbot of the Præmonstratensians, and Chaplain to the Roman Pontiffs.
3. John Grauncorth, amiable to God and man; who in his days was as illustrious in our order as Lucifer and Hesperus in the heavens. Ruled 19 years, 89 weeks.
4. Hugh de Lincoln. Ruled 18 years, 6 months.
5. Simon. Ruled 5 years, 12 days.
6. Laurence. Ruled 16 years, 8 months.
7. Richard de Normanton, "who was a delapidator in his time and very burdensome to his successors." He ruled 8 years the first time, a few days excepted.
8. John de Lincoln. Ruled 6 years.
9. Richard de Normanton. Ruled 1 year, 38 weeks.
10. John Horsley. Governed 26 years, 40 weeks. Being worn out with age he resigned his power into the hands of the convent.
11. John Wodhouse. Ruled 15 weeks.
12. William Horsley. In his days the stone chamber was built at Stanley Grange, and many other most substantial buildings erected. He ruled 21 years, 41 weeks.
13. Roger de Kyrketon. Ruled 8 years, 88 weeks.
14. William de Boney (? Bonly). Repaired several edifices which were in a ruinous state. Ruled 42 years, 18 weeks.
15. Henry Monyasche. Ruled 39 years, 11 weeks.
16. John Spondon. Ruled 33 years. "And he built the roof of the body of the church, and erected the chapel of the Blessed Virgin Mary, where the antiphon is sung on Sundays. On whose soul may God have mercy. Amen."
17. John Stanley. "Caused the cloister of our abbey to be built, and acquired by his prudence and labour, certain lands and tenements that had been lost in ancient times. He ruled 22 years, and afterwards departed to the Lord."
18. Richard Potyngham (? Notyngham). "He made the roof to the high choir, raised various edifices, and performed many benefits to this monastery. And like a good shepherd happily governed the

sheep committed to his charge, and then, his soul being freed from the body, he ended his life in peace."

" ccc.xl.iij. years, ix. weakes, and xx. dayes."

" The Abbey founded in or about 1204 by William de Hanselin, and William de Grendon (vide chron. xii.), was surrendered to the crown 20 October, 1539, when the revenues were estimated at £144 4s. per annum. Willis says that it was surrendered by John Stanton, the last abbot, and sixteen monks ; but Lysons says, ' It appears by the commissioners' accounts of that date that John Bedo, the last abbot, had a pension of £26 13s. 4d., and fifteen monks various smaller pensions.' "—*Glover*.

The following list of monks and other persons connected with the Abbey is extracted from the original Pension Roll of Philip and Mary, Addit. MSS., 8102, Brit. Mus., all of whom were living in 1553. As no mention occurs here of either John Stanton or John Bede, they may have died before this Pension Roll was made.

" Com : Derbie

Dale, nuper monasterium
{ Ffeod :
  Annat :
  Peno :

Ffeod : { Henrici Sacheverell et Willi filii sui Capitalis Senescall omnium posses- sionum dict. nup. monasterii p. ann. xxvj^s viij^d

Ann^{ts}
Edwardi Thacker et Thom. Thacker, p. ann : liij^s iv^d
Ade Bardesey als Bardesley p. ann. xl^s
Radi Hanke p. ann. xx^s
Rici Powtrell p. ann xx^s

Radi Haryson p. ann. c^s
Johannis Cadman p ann. cvj^s viij^d
Johnis Bank, p ann. c^s
Ricardi Wheteley p ann cvj^s viij^d
Jacobi Cleyton p. ann. xl^s
Georgii Cooke p. ann. c^s
Ricardi Halstamo p ann cvj^s viij^d
Johannis Shelmefeld p ann lxvj^s viij^d
Johannis Bateman p. ann xl^s
Roberti Gerard p ann xvj^s viij^d
Jacobi Conyhelme p ann. lxvj^s viij^d "

There is a full account of the valuations of the goods, etc., of Dale Abbey, Addit. MSS., 6698, p. 529, Brit. Mus.

DEEDS RELATIVE TO THE DONATIONS TO DALE ABBEY.

1. William the son of Radulph grants to Galfrid de Salicosa Mara, and to Matilda, wife of Galfrid, his own daughter, and to their heirs, his domain of Stanley, in consideration of £100 sterling paid to him by the said Galfrid and his wife.

2. William the son of Radulph grants to Serlo de Grendon and to his heirs, the wood of Okebrook called the Small Haye, adjoining the park of Thomas Bardolph, in order to convert it into a park for himself, with all the royalties which it derived from a royal charter.

3. Galfrid de Salicosa Mara confirms to the monastery the whole

donation which Serlo de Grendon had made of his land of Ockbrook, subject to forensic service only.

4. William de Grendon for the love of God, and for the salvation of his own soul, and of the souls of Serlo, his father, and of Margaret, his mother, and of Jordan and Fulcher, his brothers, and for the souls of his ancestry and posterity, gives, grants, and confirms to God, the church of the Blessed Mary, of Stanley Park, and the Canons of the Præmonstratensian order, the whole of his land of Okebrook with all that appertains thereto in pure and perpetual gift.

5. Then follows the deed of Galfrid de Salicosa Mara, and of Matilda, his wife, concerning the lordship of Depedale. It runs thus :—

"To all the faithful in Christ, now and evermore, health. You may understand that we Galfrid de Salicosa Mara and Matilda my wife the daughter of William, son of Radulph sometime seneschal of Normandy, have granted, and by this deed confirmed to God, to the church of Blessed Mary of Stanley Park and to the Abbot and Canons of the Præmonstatentian order serving God in that place, the whole donation which William de Grendon made to the said church by his deed of free and perpetual gift: viz., the lordship of Depedale with all its appurtenances and liberties, and six shillings of annual payment, which the said William was accustomed to demand by tributary right for six bovates of land in Okebrooke, in the possession of F. de Wybarville as the deed of the said William testifies, etc."

Then follows the charter of 19 Hen. III., A.D. 1235, confirming the donations of various pious persons to this house, signed by the hand of the Bishop of Chichester, the chancellor, at Burton, the 11th of September.

I believe a movement is about to be made to restore the old chapel (or parish church) of Dale. No true antiquary, however good a churchman, could possibly desire such a thing. It is unique, and nothing whatever could be done, without removing so much that is interesting. My advice is to let the old church alone : keep it in good repair, but let it alone. If a more commodious church is required, why not rebuild the choir of the abbey church on its old foundations? Incorporate the old window, which has so long been such an object of wonder and interest, place in the building every relic found in the recent excavations (the old tiles would form a glorious pavement for the sanctuary), and then there would be a church at Depedale worthy of the place. There would be no lack of funds, I am persuaded, for there is no man in Derbyshire at all proud of his county who would not be glad to make some offering for this good work. A little organisation in the county would be required, no doubt, but the work *could be accomplished ;* and it would indeed reflect great credit on the age, if it could hand down to future generations a monument like this, as an act of reparation for the long and unholy desecration of the place where saints have prayed, and where so many bodies of God's children await the Day of Resurrection.

REPRINTED FROM THE "RELIQUARY, QUARTERLY ARCHÆOLOGICAL JOURNAL AND REVIEW." EDITED BY LLEWELLYNN JEWITT, F.S.A.

www.ingramcontent.com/pod-product-compliance
Lightning Source LLC
Chambersburg PA
CBHW020626260626
47157CB00009B/3198